T0132477

The Tales of Nana Nini . . .

Nana Knows

SUSAN EDIE ASHE

AuthorHouse™
1663 Liberty Drive
Bloomington, IN 47403
www.authorhouse.com
Phone: 1 (800) 839-8640

© 2019 Susan Edie Ashe. All rights reserved.

No part of this book may be reproduced, stored in a retrieval system, or transmitted
by any means without the written permission of the author.

Published by AuthorHouse 08/07/2019

ISBN: 978-1-7283-0471-7 (sc)
ISBN: 978-1-7283-0470-0 (e)

Library of Congress Control Number: 2019903287

Print information available on the last page.

Any people depicted in stock imagery provided by Getty Images are models,
and such images are being used for illustrative purposes only.
Certain stock imagery © Getty Images.

This book is printed on acid-free paper.

Because of the dynamic nature of the Internet, any web addresses or links contained in this book may have changed
since publication and may no longer be valid. The views expressed in this work are solely those of the author and do
not necessarily reflect the views of the publisher, and the publisher hereby disclaims any responsibility for them.

authorHOUSE®

The Tales of Nana Nini . . .

Nana Knows

Table of Contents

Dedication

This book is dedicated to my
Grandchildren,
Eve, Henrik and Wyatt.
I love you and hope you enjoy this book
as much as I loved writing it for you.

Nana Nini's Life Lessons

1. The Golden Rule: treat others as you would like to be treated.
2. There is more to life than just me. I was made for more.
3. It makes me feel good to help others.
4. If it is to be, it is up to me.
5. Team work is dream work.
6. Prior planning prevents poor performance.

Nana Knows You're... Sparkle-worthy

Chapter 1

"Who wants to go with me on an adventure? We'll drive up the mountain to Sedona to get my horses, Donny and Marie," Nana asked her grandkids. They were all sitting in Nana's great room in front of a large window with the Superstition Mountains in view. Nana sitting on her sofa, her grey hair slightly messy, was wearing her favourite outfit. The blue blouse, covered with dog hair, also complemented her pleasantly plump figure.

"Why Nana?" Eden asked.

"We will bring them down to the Valley so we can ride them," Nana explained. "I love baby-sitting you guys. I have you all to myself and you are a captive audience and I can teach you my Life Lessons."

"Good idea, Nana." Eden answered while petting Roxy as she slept on the rug. "I love riding in the Moxymobile, especially when we stop for ice cream. I think I was smart to make up the name, Moxymobile, as a combination of Murphy's and Roxy's names."

"You're by far, my smartest grand daughter," Nana declared.

"Nana, I am you're only grand daughter!" Eden was also Nana's oldest grandchild. With her medium brown hair, blue-grey eyes and tons of freckles, she reminded her Grandma of Dora the Explorer. Today she was wearing her favorite color, purple. Eden loved dogs and enjoyed being the Princess, trying to make everyone obey her at all times. Nana told Eden, "You are too cute for words," many times, creating a special bond between the two females.

"I do," Murphy replied. "I have to help you drive the Moxymobile."

Murphy was one of Nana's 'furry' grandchildren. Nana had rescued him from a dog shelter and was a Dandie Dinmot terrier. Frequently wagging his big, bushy brown tail, he had never met a stranger. Murphy considered himself the man of the group, he was the alpha male. It was his job to protect and defend the household. Both dogs could talk because Nana brought back magic flowers from Costa Rica, which the dogs accidently ate before Nana could stop them.

"I'm scared," Roxy mumbled. "I might meet someone mean. Didn't you say we will stop at a dog park along the way?" Roxy was another of Nana's 'furry' grandchildren. She too was a rescue dog. Roxy, her black tail tucked between her legs, was shy and afraid of everything. She was an Affenpincher mix, but was the opposite of this ancient breed, since she avoided confrontation whenever possible.

"Yes," said Murphy. "But I told you there is nothing to be afraid of whenever you meet another dog or person."

"I know you told me," Roxy said. "But they are so big and have huge teeth and worst of all they smell my butt."

"Roxy, that is the way dogs greet each other," Eden explained.

"Can't they high five me or something?" Roxy questioned.

"Be brave," Eden counselled. "Look them in the eye and have a positive attitude. Don't let them bully you."

"She's right," Murphy replied. "Roxy, I will help you if you get in trouble. Remember guys, don't ever let anyone dull your sparkle."

"You are sparkle worthy. OK gang, time to go to bed. But, first let me read to you," Nana said sitting on Eden's bed with a pink and purple quilt, a true Princess castle. Several pictures filled the walls of horses and the actor Zac Efron. Roxy was lying at the foot of the bed, with Murphy curled up on the rug.

"Good night my love, good night.

Sweet dreams my love, tonight,

Now it's time to sleep..."

After finishing the lullaby, Nana threw kisses to everyone. "See you kiddos in the morning. Love you."

"Night, Nana. I love you SO much," Eden said. "You are the best Nana in the WORLD."

"Ditto," Murphy and Roxy replied in unison.

Nana kissed everyone one more time and left for the night.

"What fun, we get to go with Nana on a trip tomorrow. This will be an exciting adventure," Eden explained to Murphy and Roxy while lying in her bed. "We are driving up the mountain to get Nana's horses in Sedona. What can go wrong? It will be fun, a simple and quick trip riding in her SUV. I like to pretend I am Amy Fleming from *Heartland* on *Netflix* and can work wonders with Nana's horses, especially Marie."

Chapter 2

Early the next morning, Nana woke everyone, and they loaded the Moxymobile. Being prepared, Nana packed anything they might need in case of emergencies. On this trip, they were towing a horse trailer for Nana's horses, Donny and Marie. Marie was a beautiful ginger coloured mare and Donny was a small black pony. Nana likes nicknames for everyone and everything. The horse trailer she called Happy Trails. Nana boarded her horses at her friend's house in Sedona, Arizona. With the Moxymobile loaded with Nana's 'stuff' and the matching trailer, Nana and the kiddos eagerly started the trip up the highway towards the red rocks in the area around Sedona.

"I love living in the desert, I especially like to observe the changes in the terrain as we drive up the Interstate to Sedona," Nana told the gang. The mountains looked purple against the desert browns and greens with a bright blue sky. The Saguaros looked like skinny green people marching up the mountain, huge white clouds dotted the cobalt blue sky.

"I like to think of us as the Nana Nini Wagon Train, a small dot on the road. Ok my P P's, are you ready to rock-and-roll?" Nana asked as she drove the Moxymobile, zigging and zagging on the windy road.

Roxy whispered, "Why does she call us P Ps again?"

"Because Nana loves to use nicknames," replied Murphy. "She likes Pleasantly Plump for herself and mine is Perfect Prince."

"I am the Precious Princess," Eden yelled.

"What is my nickname again?" Roxy asked.

"You are the Pee Pee and Poo Poo Princess."

"Eeeeuuuuwwwww."

"I can't help it sometimes," Roxy admitted.

"Don't listen to them, Roxy, you are my Cutie Patootie," Nana gushed.

"Thanks, Nana," Roxy said.

"I'm bored. Are We There Yet? I'm hungry. Can't I look at videos or play games on my iPad? That's what all my friends do in a car," Eden pouted. "I want to use my cell phone!"

"It's only a short two-hour drive. And you know, I like to spend time with my kiddos. Nana Nini's my name, spoilin' kiddos my game," Nana said. "Let's sing along with the radio, that will pass the time."

"You ain't nuthin' but a hounddog..... That is from the one and only Elvis Presley. Or how about..." Nana asked. "And they called it puppy looveeeee.... That is from one of my early crushes, Donny Osmond. I named my horse after him."

"As if," Eden mumbled as she rolled her eyes. "That is like so embarrassing. What will my friends think?"

"Quiet, she will hear you," Roxy said.

"I don't like her singing either. At least no one can hear her with the windows rolled up. And I can say whatever I want, I am the navigator. I need to help her drive. My job is to protect all the little ladies. So make me," Murphy growled.

"No, YOU make me!" Roxy stated.

"You better be quiet, BOOGERBREATH."

"No, you better be quiet, BOOGERBUTT!"

"There will be no fighting in this car," Nana yelled as she pulled the SUV over to the side of the road. "Don't make me put you on the top of the vehicle. Like Aunt Edna from one of my favorite movies, *Vacation.*"

"Ah, Nana, you would never do that to your precious babies!" Eden declared.

"You're right, that was just an idle threat," Nana said. "But I want you to behave in the vehicle. Don't rain on my parade. Oops, some suitcases fell off the top of the vehicle," Nana said. "You guys, please go out there and pick them up."

After pulling over to the side of the road, Roxy trotted over to where all the clothes, scattered along the side of the road, made a mess. "Look at the size of those Granny panties. They are huge," Roxy yelled. She pulled off the clothing using her teeth. Murphy walked around and picked up all of Nana's underwear by putting his head through them; it was Christmas time with the coloured panties around his neck.

When they finished picking up the scattered clothes, the dogs brought them back to the Moxymobile. Soon Nana had all the suitcases back on the top of the vehicle. "Sorry about that kiddos. Just a minor problem. The rest of the trip will be perfect. Sedona here we come," Nana shouted as they drove off into the wild blue yonder.

Chapter 3

The caravan swayed on the highway; the terrain changing as they drove away from the desert valley. The scenery was large rock formations and Pinon pine trees, instead of cacti and gravel. Nana continued singing, but now she whispered the lyrics she loved. "For purple mountain majesties..... above the fruited plains..."

"Guys, shall we stop at Slide Rock State Park for some fun?" Nana inquired of the group.

"Is it like the water park we always go to, Nana?" Eden asked.

"It's a natural water slide formed by Oak Creek. I have gone there since I was your age Eden," Nana explained. "It's not too far from where the horses are stabled at Miss Cathy's house."

"Okey dokey," Murphy said. "Sounds like fun."

"Nana, is the water fast? Is it cold? Will there be dogs there? You know I don't like to be around any new situations," Roxy trembled. "I might get scared. Other dogs will make fun of me or smell my butt."

"Roxy, you must think of yourself as brave, I know you can do this," Nana declared. "Pretend you are an actress playing a role, as a brave dog. You are an Affenpincher dog breed and have that blood flowing in your veins."

"As you wish, Nana," Roxy mumbled.

After parking the SUV, they walked to the creek crevices, where you could sit and slide down back toward the entrance. It was a beautiful natural creek surrounded by oak trees, including small water falls. Several other groups of people were enjoying the cold rushing water. Nana changed her clothes, wearing the old-fashioned scuba diving gear. Eden changed her clothing, wanting protection from the rocks.

"Nana, I have always wondered, why do you have all that junk?" Roxy asked.

"I like to bring along everything we may need. It's one of my Life Lessons: prior planning prevents poor performance. I took a desert survival class, learning to be prepared at all times. I'm a little old lady boy scout."

"Weeellll, it is like kind of embarrassing Nana. You look---"

"Have mercy, guys. Eden, Murphy and Roxy just sit down in the rocks and the water current will carry you down. I'll follow you."

Sliding down the creek for about five minutes, everyone enjoyed it until Nana got stuck.

"OOPS. Help me guys, I can't move. Please come help me. I'm stuck and can't get up."

Eden jumped out of the crevice and grabbed Murphy and Roxy. They could barely walk back to Nana because it was so slippery and the water current was so strong.

"Nana, what can we do to help you? You are too heavy. Get rid of all of this gear," Eden yelled to Nana as she tried to push Nana out of the crevice.

"But, I don't want to leave it here, it's wrong to leave garbage and litter our beautiful environment," Nana declared. "Please think of a way you guys can work together and solve the problem."

"Murphy, I know, give an item to each of us, we can slide on down and Nana won't be stuck in the crevice," Roxy said. "We will make her lighter in the water and she will slide down easier."

"You speak truth to power, Roxy," Nana replied. "That will work. Remind me of this situation the next time I want ice cream! Or cake or pie or cookies!"

The three amigos working together distributed the extra items, so Nana could continue down the creek with the kiddos sometimes pushing her along the way.

Back at the entrance near the parking lot Nana declared, "Wow, that was fun. Let's do it again. Thank you so much for helping me out, you guys are awesome."

"Ah, maybe not. Once was enough. I like the water park we always go to better," Eden decided. "I was kind of embarrassed about how you looked."

"Ah shucks," Nana chuckled. "It is not important how one looks on the outside, just how good you are inside. Thank you guys again for helping me out. What lesson did you learn just now?"

"Little old ladies should not do embarrassing things in public? In front of her grandchildren?" The kiddos asked in unison.

"As if! I was looking for a response about how it is good to help others," Nana explained.

"Oh, I get it. We stopped thinking of only our fun and attempted to help you," Eden said.

"BINGO! You guys were great. The lesson learned is: you all worked together as a team and solved the problem by helping me. Team work is dream work."

"Whatever... Just so that doesn't happen again," Eden said.

"There won't be a next time, kiddos, I've got this. You can trust me. We will make it to Sedona with no more problems, believe me. Remember, I am Nifty Nana."

Chapter 4

"Dudes, that was totally awesome," Nana beamed to the kiddos as they drove away from Oak Creek. "I feel energized. Let's go to the dog park before we get the horses."

"Ah Nana, I think I will pass," Roxy mumbled. "I'll just stay in the car and rest."

"Now Roxy," Murphy replied. "I told you there is nothing to be afraid of at the park. Just think of any scary dog with Nana's big Granny panties around their necks. You can't fear someone who looks like that. And remember, never let anyone dull your sparkle."

Nana and the kiddos drove to the dog park in Sedona, with the Moxymobile weaving back and forth on the road. When they arrived, Murphy and Eden walked into the park filled with several dogs. Roxy followed with her tail tucked under her legs and her head almost touching the ground. Nana, still at the car looking for the leashes, put her purse on the hood of the car.

Suddenly a dusty, dirty teenager took Nana's purse off the vehicle, running down the street.

"What are you doing? Give that back. Kiddos, stop him!" Nana yelled. Murphy and Roxy, cornered the teen by a tree; growling and barking and nipping at his feet.

Eden, running back to the car, yelled, "What are you doing? Give Nana her purse. It doesn't belong to you. I have a black belt in karate! Don't make me use it!"

"Young man, I think you have some explaining to do. Who are you and why did you try to take my purse?" Nana questioned.

The teenager's head hung down, and he sniffled, "My name is Ryan and I am just so hungry and wanted to get something to eat," the teen mumbled. "I didn't think, I reacted."

"All you had to do was ask," Nana replied. "I would have given you something to eat. It is not right to steal from someone."

"Sorry Grams," Ryan mumbled as he handed Nana's purse back to her.

"Would you like me to call your parents and tell them where you are?"

"Not really."

Murphy and Roxy continued growling and nipping at Ryan's feet.

"Yikes, stop it, you will ruin my new sneakers. I am not afraid of these wimpy dogs," Ryan declared.

Eden screamed, "Don't you dare hurt my Nana or my dogs, they are not wimpy."

"If I give you some money, will you call your parents?" Nana asked. "I don't want to interfere. I want to help you."

"Whatever..." Ryan replied.

"Promise?" Nana asked. "I want to do what's best for you and your situation."

"I promise," Ryan said.

After Nana handed him some money, Ryan ran off, mumbling, "thanks Grams."

The kiddos gathered with Nana around the Moxymobile. Nana said "Jeepers, that was scary, but I am so proud of everyone. You guys were Spunky!"

"Eden, I wasn't aware you took karate?" Nana asked.

"I was Excellent Eden! Anddd... I kind of watched a *You Tube* video about karate, Nana."

"Well, that's a creative way to solve the problem, but the truth is always the best way to go. Did anyone learn a lesson from this?" Nana asked.

"I can be strong and brave," Roxy said. "I was Roaring Roxy."

"I can be smart and think of a way to solve the problem," Murphy said. "I was Mighty Murphy."

"I can be smart, strong and brave. We worked together as a team and solved a problem," Eden said. "I was Excellent Eden."

"You guys learned another of my Life Lessons. If it is to be, it is up to me. My kiddos helped me and you worked as a team."

"It was awesome, I feel so brave now. I have something to do, Nana, I will be right back," Roxy exclaimed, hearing the theme from *Gone With the Wind* coming from a car radio. Roxy walked over to a large rock. She took a deep breath and stood up on her back legs, raising her paw to the sky. "With Nana as my witness, I will never be scared again!" Roxy roared to the sky. With her head held high and a confident flip of her tail, she pranced back to the SUV with the words of Katy Perry's song, *Hear Me Roar,* in her head.

Chapter 5

Everyone was quiet after the excitement at the dog park. They drove in the Moxymobile to Miss Cathy's home on the top of a small knoll, enjoying the vista of Sedona. The red rocks looked so beautiful against the bright blue sky, the various colors of red surrounded by green Ponderosa pine trees. Shades of pink, mauve and rose, contrasted with the bright blue of the vehicle.

"Look kiddos that rock formation, the locals call Snoopy. Don't you think it looks like Snoopy lying down and looking up at the sky?"

"Who is Snoopy?" Eden asked.

"You know from the cartoon? **Peanuts,** Lucy, Pig Pen, Charlie Brown?" Nana asked.

"Oh yeah, but it totally looks like a bunch of boring, brown rocks," Eden sniffed.

"Good grief," Nana answered.

"I am beyond bored, Nana. When will we get to Miss Cathy's? I want to see Marie and pretend I am Amy Fleming," Eden said.

"Say what?" Murphy asked.

"Never mind. Nana, when do we get to visit with Hunter in Denver?" Eden asked. "My cousin is sooo cute, even if he is a boy."

"We will visit with Hunter soon, he's old enough now to go with us on road trips," Nana explained. "And his brother, Wade, will be joining us in a few years."

"Aren't they lucky?" Eden snarked.

"Hey now, I love having you join me on road trips. You guys are a captive audience and I can share my Life Lessons with you. I thought you guys enjoyed going with me on trips?" Nana asked. "Remember, Nana Nini's my name, spoilin' kiddos my game."

"Weeellll... After today---"

"Well, exxxcuuse me. Here we are. Look there is Miss Cathy with my horses in the arena," Nana said.

"So how was the trip?" Cathy asked, walking over from the barn. "Were there any problems along the way? I expected you hours ago. And how did you ever see anything when driving that vehicle, Nini? You guys look like a wagon train with all those vehicles you haul."

Nana and the kiddos all looked at each other with wide eyes.

"Oh, everything was fine," Nana explained. "The Moxymobile can do anything. I'm an excellent driver and packer. There were no problems at all."

"Naaannnaaa!"

"Tell her about all the Granny panties around my neck---"

"Tell her about how brave I was," Roxy roared---

"Tell her about how we helped you get unstuck at Slide Rock..."

"Tell her about how embarrassed we were---"

"Tell her about how we saved you from the teenager!"

Nana Knows You're... Gold-worthy

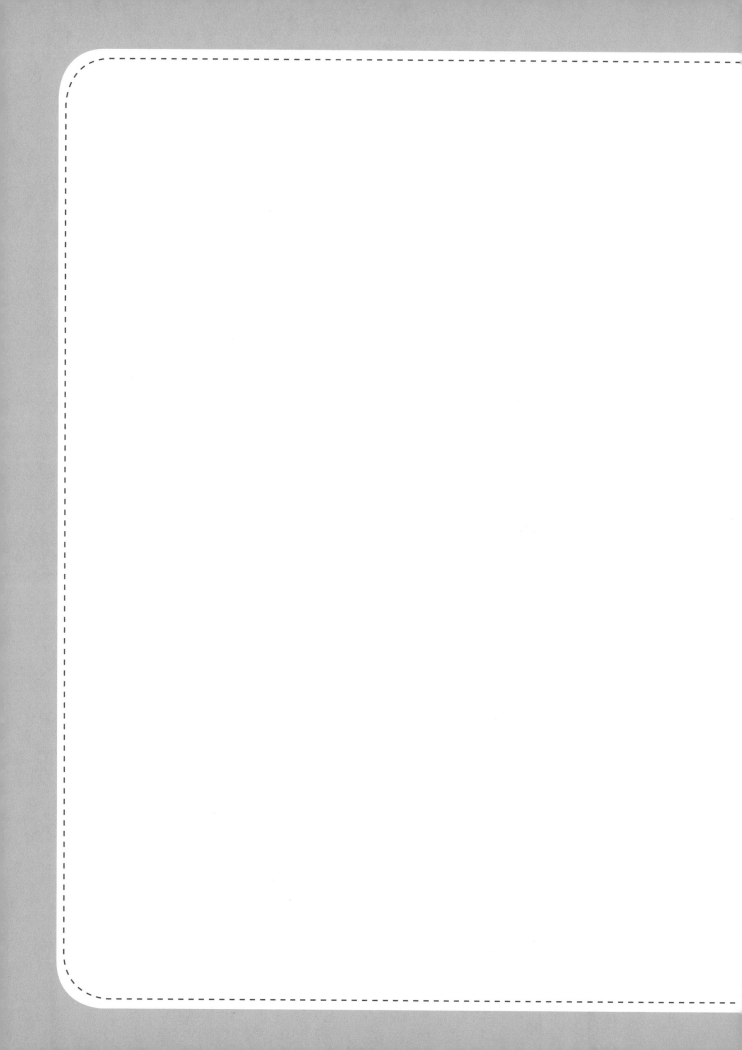

Chapter 1

"Who wants to go look for buried treasure with me, like Indiana Jones? We will camp near the Superstition Mountains." Nana questioned everyone as they sat in the living room watching the Arizona sunset outside the large picture window. Eden was Nana's human granddaughter. Her medium length brown hair contrasted with Roxy's black fur. They were sitting on the rug combing each other's hair. Roxy and Murphy are Nana's 'furry' grandchildren. Murphy looked out the window and growled at a jackrabbit staring back at him. His paw and brown tail pointed towards the Palo Verde tree outside where the rabbit jumped to safety. The various cacti covered Nana's yard with the shades of green contrasting with the mauve-colored rocks.

"Who is Indiana Jones?" Eden questioned.

"He is a character in the movies and his life is full of exciting adventures, just like we enjoy on our road trips," Nana explained.

"Never heard of him," Eden yawned.

Truth be told, Eden loved watching 'her' movies, especially all the Disney Princesses. Elsa was her favorite from the movie *Frozen.* Boring 'boy' movies were too noisy for her tastes.

"Your Papa and Uncle loved going to see him in the movies when they were your age," Nana responded.

"Big whoop," Eden replied. "They are old, but just not as old as you, Nana. No one is as old as you are."

"I 'm a wild and crazy gal," Nana sniffed to Eden as she arranged her gray curls around her face. "Remember, I prefer 'seasoned' instead of old and 'pleasantly plump' instead of fat. Do you realize you too will be old one day?"

"As if," the gang replied in unison.

"As if yourself," Nana said as she deeply sighed.

Eden and Roxy continued grooming each other on the floor, as Murphy stared outside. He knew his job was to protect everyone in the house. Even though he was just a dog, he knew he was the man of the house; in his mind at least. So far he had protected the gals from all kinds of scary characters, especially the one in the brown truck who came to the house all the time. Nana was always buying stuff on the internet she HAD to have for any road trips the gang took together.

Nana said, "Mi Amigos, I want to take you guys camping in the Superstition Mountains, so we can find buried gold and be rich and famous, even though it is about ten miles from here."

"Grreattt, sounds like fun," Murphy mumbled.

"OooKaaaay," Roxy and Eden said.

"Hey, you guys don't sound excited, I feel the negativity in this room," Nana challenged.

"Nana, we have done things with you before, remember?" Roxy replied.

"Hey, have we ever had any problems?" Nana questioned.

"Yes!" Murphy replied, "Remember when you got stuck in the crevice on the creek and a teenager tried to take your purse?"

"Oh yeah, I forgot about that," Nana said. "OK, did anyone EVER get hurt at ANY time?"

"Yes!"

"Well, OK was there blood?" Nana responded.

"Yes!"

"Oops, a lot of blood?"

"Well, not actually a lot---" Roxy declared.

"OK, there you go," Nana replied. "It could have been worse."

"Yes, Nana..."

"There are days I regret finding that magic flower in Costa Rica, allowing you guys to talk," Nana revealed.

"Nana, you always told us we are extra special 'cause we can talk," Roxy exclaimed.

"You're special," Nana replied. "For many reasons. Being able to talk is just one way we bond with each other. I hope no one else got into the flowers

I accidentally threw out. There may be other animals out there who can talk too."

"Alright then, let's move on and get back to my story. How about pretending we are Cap'n Jack Sparrow then?" Nana asked.

"Now you're talking Nana. I think he is so handsome," Roxy swooned.

"Me too," Nana and Eden shouted at the same time.

"Actually, Johnny Depp is one of my many pretend boyfriends," Nana admitted.

"Where are we going to find an ocean and pirate ship in Arizona?" Murphy questioned. "In the desert full of cacti?"

"Are we going to Canyon or Saguaro Lake?" Eden asked.

Nana and the gang loved being outdoors and enjoying all the beauty Arizona offered. A lake in the middle of the desert surrounded by cacti is unique. The Saguaro cacti, tall with long skinny arms looked like they were marching down the mountain and about to jump into the lake.

"I said pretend like we are Indiana Jones or Captain Jack," Nana said. "Anyway, I thought we could pack up the vehicles and horses and go camping in the mountains. We will go to the lake sometime soon, maybe go kayaking and see the wild horses."

Nana owned many vehicles to help her and the gang when they went on trips. The Moxymobile was strong enough to haul her many vehicles. *Nana's Nook* was a glamorous vintage camper, with a fancy chandelier over the bed. She used it to go 'glamping'. Her horse trailer was fancy too and was color coordinated with the Moxymobile. Donny and Marie, her horses, traveled in style. Nana liked nicknames, and she called the trailer *Happy Trails.*

"Actually, I like riding your pretty mare, Marie. Donny is just a puny little pony for babies," Eden said.

"We'll take turns," Nana suggested.

"So, how do you really know if there is any gold in the Superstition Mountains?" Murphy questioned.

"Ah, I have done research and found old maps to help me. And there are several legends about what happened in the Supes or Superstitions. But no one knows what really happened; you need to decide what is true or false. It will be fun," Nana replied.

Nana and the gang continued talking as they walked toward Eden's princess bedroom. It was time to get ready for bed.

"Actually, all mountains look big and scary, with all kinds of animals living there!" said Roxy, as she thought about the Superstitions. "I think I may stay at camp."

"Now Roxy," Nana said, "Remember you are brave and capable of going on the adventures with us. You are Sparkle-worthy and Amazing-worthy! You're made of pure gold! Remember to think of everyone wearing HUGE Granny panties around their necks. No one can hurt or scare you with silly Granny panties around their necks. Roaring Roxy Rules!"

"If you say so Nana," Roxy mumbled. "Murphy looked so silly when that happened."

Everyone settled into Eden's bedroom with Roxy laying at the bottom of the bed and Murphy curled on the rug next to the bed. Nana tucked Eden into her pink and purple comforter. "Time for me to read you my lullaby." "Good night, my love good night," Nana started the lullaby and ended with "Forever and Always Nana."

"Sweet dreams, go to sleep now and tomorrow we will go find our gold. I know that nothing will go wrong on our Next Big Adventure," Nana explained. "This will be our first perfect adventure. I can't wait. Who wants to ride up front with me?"

"It's my turn," Roxy said.

"No, I always have to help her drive," Murphy declared.

"I am the Princess, I always get to ride in the front, besides I am her favorite,"Eden pronounced.

"EEddeennnn!"

Chapter 2

After watching a beautiful sunrise surround the Superstition mountains with vibrant colors from Nana's window, everyone piled into the Moxymobile. They packed it with everything possibly needed for the trip. Driving along the highway when the Moxymobile turned a corner, everything shifted and the desert animals watched in fear. The camper and horse trailer followed behind the MM, swaying in unison. It looked like an old-fashioned wagon train going along the road; the Nana Knows Trail instead of the Santa Fe Trail.

"Here we go again, another road trip, yippee kay oh!" Nana yelled. *On the Road Again,* by Willie Nelson was blaring on the radio.

"Dude, be strong, we will get through this new adventure with Nana," Murphy said from the backseat, his front paws on the console. "Remember, Nana likes to spend time with us, she loves us and wants us to grow up to be strong adults. She talks about her Life Lessons all the time."

"Snotty sneakers, I am up to my eyeballs with all these positive thoughts," Roxy moaned.

"Ditto," Murphy and Eden groaned.

Arriving at the base of the Superstitions, Eden helped Nana set up camp. With all of Nana's essentials to unpack, it took the gals a couple of hours to make the camp feel like home.

Later in the day, while hiking along the trails, everyone enjoyed the beauty of the mountains and the clear blue sky filled with white puffy clouds. It was a Chamber of Commerce kind of day, Arizona style.

While watching the sun set, causing the Superstitions to turn red, Nana prepared a meal ending with s'mores in front of a huge bonfire. Munching on the last marshmellows, everyone was full, so they quickly cleaned up and settled down around the camp.

"OK, want to hear the story of the Lost Dutchman? And the gold and the secret mine?" Nana asked.

"Was it like in the movies? Like Indiana Jake or Captain John?" Roxy asked. "Yes, and that's Indiana Jones and Captain Jack," Nana replied.

"Whatever..."

"Jumping Gehospath, you guys are, shall we say, underwhelmed with an interest in the story of this adventure," Nana pouted.

"I want to play video games and text my friends, Nana," Eden seethed.

Nana was used to the lack of enthusiasm her grand kids showed on a daily basis. With her positive look on life, she looked beyond this attitude and continued sharing her Life Lessons, experiences and stories to the kiddos.

"And aaawwwway we go," Nana said. "The Saga of the Superstitions. It has legends, treasure maps, mystery, disappearances and murder. And most important, lots of gold worth lots of money. Truthfully, no one knows for sure what really happened. It is a mystery and many people have tried to find the answers," Nana starts.

"But do you know where the gold is?" Eden asks.

"I know where some gold is, not THE gold," Nana admitted.

"Here is my special buried treasure map," Nana said, showing the gang a piece of paper full of symbols. "Just like in the movies or the olden days, we need to follow it to find the gold. It happened somewhere in these mountains behind us. People think the goldmine may be around Weaver's Needle. The problem is the area is filled with narrow canyons and nearly vertical cliffs, hundreds of feet high covered with cacti."

Nana, warming up to sharing this story with the Three Amigos, noticed everyone was leaning closer to hear her better.

"A long time ago, in the mid-1840's, the United States was ending the Spanish American War. During this time a man from Mexico, Don Peralta, explored the Superstition Mountains looking for a gold mine. Eventually, the Apaches living in the area murdered his entire group in a three-day battle. This was their land, and they did not like people trespassing on their land. The Apaches did not want the gold and threw it on the trail. More important to them, were the rifles and animals the Spaniards had. Can you see how different cultures have contrasting values? Isn't that interesting?"

"Toys, bones, sticks and treats make my world go round!" Murphy declared.

"Double Ditto," Roxy declared.

"Money, iPads, cell phones and video games are super important," Eden revealed. "They are the basics of life."

"Tisk, Tisk, Tisk, you guys are SHAMEFUL," Nana dismayed. "Back to the story. Years later, a man called Jacob Walzer, or the Lost Dutchman, found gold mines in the area. Legend says he killed some Mexican prospectors to get the gold. He made maps showing where the gold was, but he died before the mines where located. People have been trying to figure out these maps for years. And to this day, no one has found these gold mines. It is an unsolved mystery."

"Awesome, I can imagine him and a pony like Donny full of gold walking on a trail right behind us," Murphy said. "That was a long time ago, how did you get your maps, Nana?"

"I bought them at a gift shop in Apache Junction," Nana said.

"Are they real?" Eden asked.

"Weelll... I said I know where some gold is and we will look for it tomorrow," Nana said. "So get rested and we will go prospecting for our gold. I predict we will have no problems on this adventure. It will be our first perfect adventure."

Chapter 3

Nestled at the base of the Superstitions, Goldfield Ghost Town is where Nana and the kiddos went the next day. Originally, it was a town where gold had been mined in the late 1800's. Now a ghost town and a tourist attraction, it offered fun things to do. The buildings were still there, with some of the original equipment used to mine the gold. Riding the train around the area, Murphy pretended he was the conductor. Murphy pointed out the shooting gallery and the zip line over the area. Everyone bought candy, especially the Prickly Pear fudge. Ice cream from the general store tasted extra sweet.

Tourists, riding horses along the trails, weaved around the Saguaro cacti in the green desert, sprinkled with wild flowers.

"Look, we can take a Jeep tour," Nana explained to the kiddos. "We can ride the 4 x 4 in the desert. Just like when we go off-roading with my ATV."

"Aahhh, maybe another time, Nana," Eden replied. "I am still sore from when we rode with you last week."

"You guys are a bunch of party poopers!" Nana pouted.

Watching a gun fight Murphy, pretended he was fighting right next to them. Eden was arrested and put into jail as everyone laughed at her behind bars. Nana and the kiddos strolled along the boardwalk, among people dressed in period clothing. Seeing a beautiful little Cocker Spaniel dog Murphy, lifted his hat and gave her a bow. Another dog saw Roxy and smiled at her; feeling brave, she smiled back. One of the gunfighters tipped his hat towards Nana and Eden. Eden closed her eyes, imagining she was alive during the heyday of the town. Images of *Little House on the Prairie* floated in her mind.

"Oohlala, did you see that cowboy look at me?" Nana asked. "He looks just like Walt Longmire! I swear Dale Evans and Roy Rogers just rode by on Trigger."

"Again, I have no idea who those humans are, so where is this gold you keep talking about Nana?" Roxy asked.

"Walter is my pretend cowboy boyfriend from *Longmire* on *Netflix*," Nana swooned. Roy and Dale were cowboy icons; Trigger was their horse."

"Inconceivable! Nana, you live in a dream world," Eden said.

"As you wish," Nana sighed. "See that building over there, we can go there and pan for some gold."

The group, walking into the room, were given pans with rocks and mud and they started to look for the gold. They separated the rocks by shaking them in water until the heavier gold fell to the bottom of the pan. After collecting what they found, everyone went outdoors.

"That is all you have to do to get some gold? What about all the mining equipment we had to bring? I have pickaxes in my backpack and they are heavy," Murphy said.

"I wanted to get you in the spirit of how the gold is mined, to 'feel' the experience," Nana said.

"How rude..." Murphy cried. "Nana, can we go and buy things with our gold?"

"Mmmmmmm... it is fool's gold or fake gold," Nana said. "It is not really worth anything."

"Naannna!" The gang yelled, "We went to all this work for something worthless?"

"Oh, get over yourselves," Nana said. "Let it Go Domino. We had fun and it was a bonding experience."

"Snotty sneakers to the max!" the amigos all yelled in unison.

"Look there is the Reptile Exhibit, shall we pet the snakes?" Murphy questioned.

"Nana, I do not like snakes or any lizards even though they are smaller than me, " Roxy screamed.

"I don't like reptiles either, they are slimy, yuck!" Eden explained.

"Awesome, I especially love the Gila Monsters. Let's go," Murphy yelled.

"Pass!" Eden, Roxy and Nana declared together.

Riding back to camp after visiting the ghost/gold town, Murphy gazed at the scenery; imagining Apache warriors charging down the mountains towards the Moxymobile.

"Nana, I am not sure I had fun today," Eden explained. "You said we would be rich and famous. You have a distant relationship with the truth."

"Let's just say I was dealing with alternative facts today."

A very quiet gang sat around the campfire that night, looking up at the sky and counting the stars. Nana retired early to her camper. Eden, Murphy and Roxy went to bed early in the tent; tired after such a long day.

"I wanted to have fun on this trip, like you said, Eden," Roxy moaned.

"What a bummer. I thought we were going to be rich and famous."

"After all, tomorrow is another day, Roxy," Murphy said. "Remembering what type of person you are inside is more important than owning gold. Sleep tight. I love you guys."

Eden, curled up in her sleeping bag, tried to talk to her friends on her cell phone, but there was no service. *What a joke, go on a trip with Nana, they said. It will be fun, they said.* She mumbled to the rocks around the campsite.

Chapter 4

The next morning, after watching the sun come up behind the mountains, the gang decided to go horseback riding. Nana rode Marie, a beautiful ginger mare with a flowing tail. Nana felt like a queen mounted on her elaborate saddle, with Glen Campbell's song ***I'm a Rhinestone Cowboy*** ringing in her ears. Her large, embellished cowboy hat shielded her from the harsh Arizona sun.

Donny could barely hold the three amigos, with Murphy standing behind Eden and Roxy in front of her on the saddle horn. While riding in the desert, the gang found a cute rabbit and decided to follow it. They rode among the cacti and desert landscape singing, Oh what a beautiful morning, oh what a beautiful day...

Suddenly, the amigos were on a trail away from Nana. Just ahead of them, they saw a huge, furry, scary looking animal. The claws were long and very sharp. It was looking right at them! It had big eyes with snot dripping from its nose. At least Donny was not scared or spooked, that was good news.

Eden said, "How can we get past this scary thing?" "Should we text Nana?"

"No, we can do this," Murphy said.

"Remember Nana's Life Lessons: If it is to be, it is up to me." Eden said.

"So? What does that mean again?" Roxy asked.

"When a job needs to be done, it is up to you to make it work," Eden explained. Do not depend on someone else doing it for you."

"So, we can handle this?" Roxy asked.

"I think so," Eden said. "What would Nana do?"

"I'm scared," Roxy said. "I don't like Big scary monsters! It has the eye of the tiger."

"What happened to Roaring Roxy?"

"That was then, this is now," Roxy explained. "Nana says I am a work in progress. I have good days and bad days. And that was before I saw this thing!!"

Just then the big monster started growling and scratched the ground with its sharp claws.

"We have to do something before he eats us," said Eden. "I know, I will tie up Donny to the tree and then go behind the boulder. Murphy and Roxy you go behind me, take the lasso and put it around his neck. I will make funny noises to get his attention, you guys can tie him up."

"Sounds like a plan," Murphy agreed.

"Hi Ho Silver, it's the Lone Ranger," Murphy yelled. "Let's roll, Tonto. Giddyup!"

"Ok, Kemo Sabe," Roxy yelled back.

"Look at me, you silly looking thing," Eden hollered, jumping up and down, making faces at the creature. "I'm not afraid of you."

While Eden yelled, Murphy and Roxy took the rope and slipped it around the neck of the monster, attaching the rope to Donny's saddle and tying it tightly. Finally, they ran to the safety of the boulder.

"Wow, this is just like in the movies. We did it," Murphy yelled.

The gang started running around in circles with their hands raised above their heads, the music from *Rocky* ringing in their heads as they did the victory laps.

Nana rode up on Marie, with clouds of dust around her. "I was so worried about you guys," Nana said. "What happened? What are you doing to that poor little coyote pup?"

"Little? He is HUGE to us. Nana, we thought he was a scary monster and we were just being brave and tied him up to save us," Murphy explained.

Nana's grandchildren crowded around her, as far away as possible from the monster.

"We used some of your Life Lessons you always share with us. If it is to be, it is up to me. Also, prior planning prevents poor performance. Your lessons helped us work together to solve the problem with the monster. Team work is dream work."

"Well, I am very proud of you guys being brave and thinking before you acted on something," Nana explained. "But, he is just a little tiny, baby coyote. You untie that poor little thing, he probably is scared to death."

"Naannaa... But we worked together as a team---"

"Let him go, we have things to do."

Feeling defeated, the gang untied the coyote and let him loose. He quickly ran away to freedom. Roxy hoped the rabbit was far away in its burrow.

"Well, I guess we finally did the right thing," Eden realized. "It didn't last long, but what fun. I felt so brave when he was finally tied up."

"I was Roaring Roxy again! Roxy rules."

"Good for you, you go girl," Nana said. "You were Mighty Murph and Excellent Eden again too. I am so proud of everyone."

"We were Cap'n Jack and Indiana Jones all rolled into one."

"Let's continue our ride and get back to our camp," Nana said. "Who wants to go and buy pretend things with our pretend gold?"

"Nannnaa..."

Chapter 5

The next morning, Nana and the kiddos worked together and broke camp. The Saguaros looking like skinny men marching down the mountains, waving goodbye to the gang.

"Wow, what an adventure you guys had," Nana babbled as she drove along the highway. "So exciting. I was so proud of everyone and how you all worked as a team. My brave babies!"

"Yuck, Nana, we are NOT babies," the gang all yelled in unison, their mouths open with their fingers inside.

"You'll always be my babies," Nana sighed. "Anyway, I was pleased how you used my Life Lessons to solve your problems."

"Yes, Nana. I was wondering," Eden said, "Why do we always have to go on road trips with you? This trip was a bummer!"

"Eden Lynne, this trip was not a bummer. You learned you have a heart made of gold; which I feel is more important that finding gold. All of you learned to work as a team and help each other," Nana continued. "There is more to life than just me; another one of my Life Lessons. Also, your parents need me to babysit, they are working to help pay my Social Security. Finally, you guys are a captive audience in the Moxymobile, forced to listen. I can't wait for our next adventure," Nana said. "Bring it on!"

"You get PAID to watch us?" Eden asked in disbelief.

"It's a long story..." Nana explained.

"Well... I was Excellent Eden still!"

"I was Mighty Murph as always!"

"I was pup of the world," Roxy whispered to herself. "I am pup of the world. I AM PUP of the WORLD!!" she yelled. "**I AM PUP OF THE WORLD.**"

Nana Knows You're... Ski-worthy

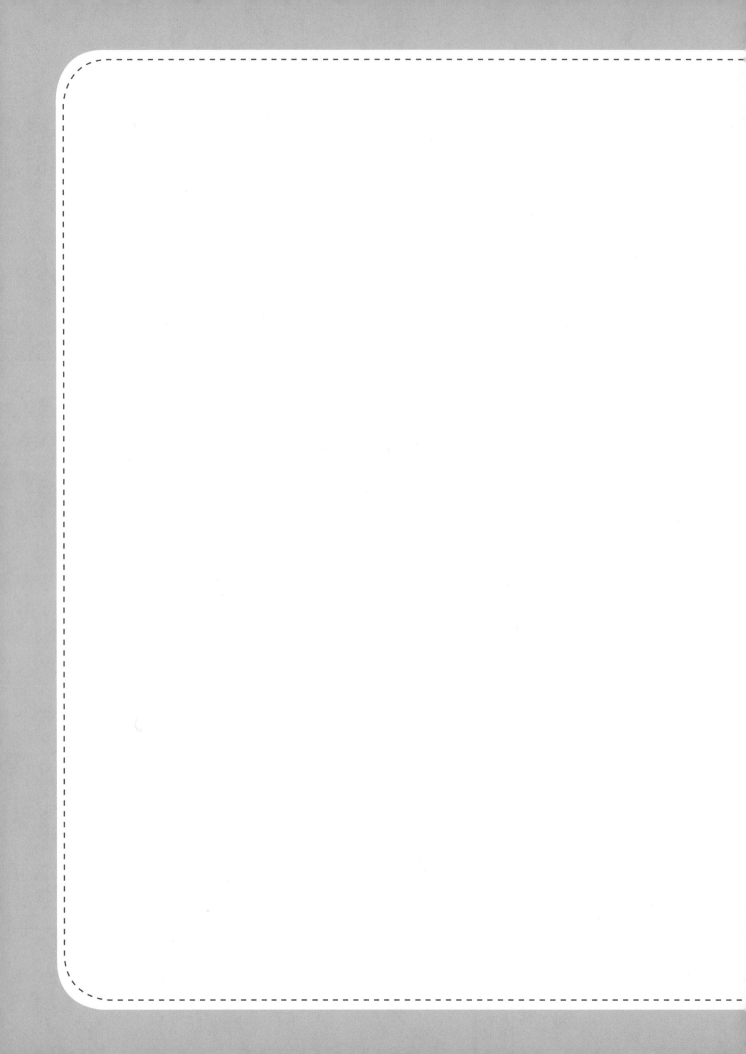

Chapter 1

"Who wants to go with me to visit Hunter, Coco and Toby in Colorado? I want to go skiing near Uncle Brandon's house," Nana asked the gang.

"I do," Murphy yelled as he wagged his brown tail.

"I do," Roxy murmured as she curled her black tail around her body.

"Me too, that's awesome," Eden replied. She loved visiting her cousins, spending time with her family, most of the time.

"I am excited to spend time with Hunter," Nana replied as they sat together watching a rare thunderstorm out the window in her living room.

"Skiing alone? With you Nana?" The amigos whispered together.

"Ruh roh, you guys don't sound very excited. Again." Nana said.

"Nana, we are seasoned travelers with you now. We know what can happen," Murphy replied.

"Unfortunately," the amigos replied in unison.

"Holy Moley. I have a somewhat good track record, no broken bones," Nana explained. "You guys need to be more positive about our adventures."

"Tomorrow is another day," the gang all yelled in unison.

"Hey now, it will be fun. Hunter is old enough to go with us. Toby and Coco are coming too," Nana said. "Your new cousin, Wade, will stay with his parents."

"Why does he get to stay with my Uncle and Aunt?" Eden demanded.

"His day will come," Nana promised.

Eden admitted, "On a brighter side, they are the coolest Colorado dog dudes. I am so glad we get to see them."

"They are WAY cooler than we are," Murphy and Roxy sighed together.

"They are pure bred dogs, Retrievers. They have bigger brains or something," Murphy moaned.

"Maybe some of it will rub off on us," Roxy sighed even louder.

"In your dreams," Eden laughed. "Wait until you meet my dog, Pixel. She is super smart. She has had a lot of training."

"I feel scared," Roxy said. "We are so out of our league."

"Yeppers," Murphy declared.

"Don't sell yourselves short," Nana said. "I am very proud of how you guys handled yourselves in the past. You followed my Life Lessons and saved the day many times. You are just as smart as any other dog, be proud of who and what you guys accomplish. Murphy, you're a Dandie Dinmot terrier, a noble dog breed. Sir Walter Scott made Dandie Dinmont's famous in a book, knowing the breed to be courageous and very intelligent. Murphy, you are multi-cultural with an Irish name and Scottish blood. Roxy, you're an Affenpinscher terrier, another noble dog breed, known to be confident and fearless. I am very proud of my babies, no matter your dog lineage."

"So be it," Murphy said as he bowed to Nana.

"Time to go Nite-Nite so we can start fresh in the morning. This time will be perfect with no problems, you'll see," Nana offered.

"Are Donny and Marie going with us this time, Nana?" Eden asked about the two horses that Nana owned. Marie was a beautiful mare and Donny was a small pony.

"Not this trip. I am excited, I have never skiied before. It will be perfect, I just know, " Nana replied.

"In YOUR dreams, Nana, you are perfect," Eden added. "However, in reality... Anyway, read us your lullaby, Nana, it makes me feel so happy and loved." Eden snuggled next to Nana as she read the poem.

"Good night my love, good night..."

After finishing the lullaby Nana said, "See you in the morning. I love you, sweet dreams."

"Good night, Nana, we love you too," the gang replied in unison.

"Who is your boyfriend?" Roxy whispered to Eden after Nana left the room.

"Zac Efron, naturally," Eden swooned. "My favorite movies are ALL the High School Musicals! And *The Greatest Showman* is awesome."

"Who is your sweetie, Murphy?" Eden inquired.

"Lady Gaga!" Murphy whispered.

"I didn't see that coming. Why?" Eden asked.

"Didn't you see her wearing a meat dress? I was drooling, thinking about it for days!" Murphy swooned.

"How typical, a male thinking only of his stomach," Eden declared.

"Unbeelievabble," Roxy agreed. "Maybe Zac will make a movie someday with my boyfriend, Tramp, from the movie, **Lady and the Tramp.**

"We can only dream, Roxy, someday our prince will come…" Eden sighed.

"Anyway, good night, sweet dreams."

"Good night, Eden and Murphy," Roxy said. "Maybe this trip will be THE perfect one with no problems."

Chapter 2

The next morning Nana and the gang worked together and packed the vehicles. They started towards Denver driving in the Moxymobile, pulling the camper, *Nana's Nook,* and the toy hauler, looking again like a wagon train from the Old West. All the vehicles weaved on the road as they climbed the mountain towards the resort; with Pine trees this time climbing up the mountains instead of the Saguaro cacti. The mountains of Colorado differ from the mountains of Arizona, but are just as beautiful. John Denver's *Rocky Mountain High* song was blaring on the radio, followed by Diana Ross' song *Ain't No Mountain High Enough.* The next afternoon, Nana and the group pulled into the driveway of her son's house. Brandon was standing there with Hunter in his arms.

"Wow, Ma, that is a lot of vehicles you are pulling. Are you SURE you can drive safely? With my son? And my dogs?" Brandon asked.

"Hey, I finally passed my driving test. I am good to go," Nana replied. "I take care of all my babies, just like I took care of you and your brother."

"Megan and I are hesitant to let you do this, but I guess we trust you," Brandon said. "Somewhat."

"This will be a perfect adventure, you have my word!" Nana promised.

"Well, call me anytime and have fun," Brandon said.

"The boy doth protest too much, me thinks," Nana responded. "We will have fun, you'll see."

After loading Hunter into the Moxymobile along with the dogs, Nana drove towards the ski resort, again enjoying the scenery.

"Hey Nana, since you are a desert rat from Arizona, doesn't the snow bother you?" Eden questioned from the front seat.

"Nah, I am WOMAN, hear me roar. I can handle anything," Nana exclaimed. "Remember, I am Nifty Nana."

"Nana, Eden looked at me funny," Roxy complained as she kicked the console from the backseat.

"No, YOU looked at ME funny," Eden challenged.

"And you kicked me, BOOGER BOY," Eden said looking at Murphy. "Nana, why can't we watch videos in the car like all my other friends?"

"No fighting in the Moxymobile. Please. How many times do I have to tell you guys this?" Nana declared. "I will put you on the roof of the MM!"

"But Nana, she---"

"Stop it. I will turn this car around right now..." Nana threatened.

"Yes, yes yes! Please take us back. I want to be with my friends," Eden yelled. "I want to look at my poster of Zac E in my room."

"Oops, the wrong empty threat to bribe you guys with, I suppose," Nana replied.

"OK OK, Nana. You know we hate that, when you put us on top of the car. Just because you saw it in a movie, doesn't mean you should do it." Roxy said. "It scares me a little."

"No worries, my bad." Nana answered. "Don't blame me, I am just a sweet little old Grannie. Nana Nini's my name, spoilin' kiddos my game."

"Barf-aroni," the gang all said in unison. "Why can't you knit and bake cookies like Meredith's Grandma?" Eden puzzled.

"Whatebs. Let me think. Just try to behave until we get to Breck," Nana said.

"Are you going to bribe us again?" Eden asked.

"Let me think..." Nana responded.

"If you behave, then I will not kiss you in public?" Nana said.

"Deal, best thing I heard all day," Murphy said.

"Best thing I have heard my whole life!" Eden yelled. "It is so embarrassing. What will my friends think?"

"I sometimes like a kiss, Nana," Roxy admitted.

"Hunter likes my kisses, Wade likes my kisses," Nana pouted. "Right, Hunter? You like your Nana's kisses?"

"Want my Mama," Hunter cried.

"They are little babies," Eden said. "They do not understand what is in store for them."

Chapter 3

Arriving at the lodge, everyone unloaded items from the vehicles onto the snowy ground. An organizational wizard, Nana liked to have all her 'stuff' with her, just in case of an emergency.

Nana and the gang walked to the beginning of the ski run, hauling all the equipment behind them. "Look there is our ski gondola. Hurry and help me load the gondola," Nana told the gang. Eden, Roxy, Murphy, Toby and Coco pushed, shoved and crammed items into the gondola; while Nana and Hunter watched and supervised.

"Nana, you have enough stuff to open your own ski shop," Murphy panted as he pushed a snowshoe into a backpack.

"I am prepared for any emergency. Prior planning prevents poor performance, is one of my Life Lessons," Nana explained.

"Nana and her lessons. She is always the teacher," Roxy said.

Suddenly the gondola takes off before Nana and Hunter can get inside. "Be careful and come back and get us," Nana yells.

Nana watching through her binoculars, sees everyone go to the top of the run and come back and stop in front of her and Hunter; she pushes Hunter into Eden's lap before the gondola takes off again.

"Come back for me," Nana yells as the gondola lurches ahead on the track. On the third try Nana gets inside the gondola with the gang and all of Nana's stuff, filling every corner of the gondola.

"'Phew, we did it!" Murphy yells.

"What now, Nana?" Eden asks.

"We all go skiing. It will be fun," Nana answered.

Scattering out onto the snow, the gang gets off the gondola and onto the bunny slope. With Hunter's snowsuit so tight, his arms stretched straight, he waddles towards his skis. Eden's ski outfit, pink and purple with matching boots and hat, contrasted with Nana's jumpsuit and hat, her walker strapped onto her skis.

"Can't move my arms, need to go pee pee, now!" Hunter cried.

After taking Hunter to the bathroom and giving him to Eden, Nana carefully moves to the Bunny run.

"I feel the need for speed," Nana yelled at the top of the small slope.

"OK, Maverick," Murphy said.

Nana, moving along the bunny slope, falls over after weaving back and forth. Landing with her skis vertical and the walker attached, her face is smashed into the snow; with her arms outstretched.

"Help, help, I've fallen and can't get up," Nana yells. "Where is everybody?"

"I am right here, Nana, what happened to I am WOMAN, hear me roar?" Eden asked. "Your ego is writing checks your body can't cash. You're too old to try all this physical stuff."

"I guess I can't handle the truth. Now the song, **I Will Survive** by Gloria Gaynor is going through my head," Nana mumbled.

"You're fine, Nana," Roxy determined. "There is no gushing blood, no broken bones."

"Great, my perfect record is still in effect, no broken bones," Nana determined. "I feel a little sore though."

"Be careful Nana," Eden said as she helped her up and dusted the snow from her face. "Why don't you and Hunter go on back to the Lodge? We will meet you there soon."

Seeing a snow rabbit, Eden and the dogs start chasing it down the hill. Toby and Coco soon become bored and ski off on another more challenging trail. The Three Amigos continue following the rabbit as he weaves in and out of the trees and rocks. Moments later, the rabbit falls into a hole and is covered with snow, trapped inside when a large boulder moved and covered the entrance, because of a small avalanche.

"Poor baby," Roxy cries. "What are we going to do? We can't leave, it may be hurt. But, I don't want to fall in the hole with him either."

"Be brave, I will think of something," Eden says. "I know, I have a dog whistle. I will use it and see if Toby and Coco hear it and can come to help us dig him out."

"I don't want to be standing here, what if we sink into the hole? I hope help comes soon," Roxy trembled.

"We will be OK," Murphy said. "Pretend you are Elsa from **Frozen**. She would know how to feel brave. Or think of Olaf wearing Nana's huge Granny panties."

"Let it go, let it go, Domino," Eden replied.

"Actually, it would be nice to see Nana right about now," Roxy moaned as she hugged herself tighter.

"Where is my Roaring Roxy?" Murphy asked.

"That was then, this is now. I'm cold. I'm thirsty. I'm wet," Roxy replied.

Toby and Coco skied up to the gang; all the dogs and Eden worked together, using the snowshoes as shovels. The boulder moved as they released the frightened animal. He scampered quickly away.

"We are all amazing! The song **Happy** by Pharrell Williams is playing in my ear buds. Listen," Coco cheered. All the kiddos moved to the music.

"We look silly with the skis getting tangled together," Eden laughed.

"Let's go tell Nana how smart we are," Murphy suggested as they started to ski back towards Breckenridge.

"Where have you guys been, I was so worried about you?" Nana questioned everyone as they walked into the room.

"We watched a bunny fall into a hole and there was a big boulder and Eden helped us and blew her dog whistle and Toby and Coco came and we rescued the scared bunny and then we came right back to tell you, Nana," Roxy explained in one breath.

Nana sobbed as she hugged everyone at once. "My heroes!"

"I was Terrific Toby."

"I was Cool Coco."

"Thank you so much for helping us," Murphy said. "You were awesome, dudes."

"Anytime, you guys are family," Toby said hearing **We Are Family,** the song from Sister Sledge drifting out from his ear buds.

"Toby and Coco used my Life Lessons!" Nana exclaimed. "Treat others as you would want to be treated. Also, it makes you feel good to help others."

"I am Roaring Roxy, still!"

"I am Mighty Murphy, at your service!"

"But I was the one who thought of my whistle," Eden proudly added. "I am Excellent Eden for Eternity."

"I am so proud of all my babies, you guys ROCK," Nana yelled.

"Nana, we like helping others. We're going out skiing again, the powder is perfect. Does anyone want to join us?" Coco asked.

"I do," Eden and Murphy yelled in unison.

Roxy and Hunter stayed with Nana in the lodge while everyone else went skiing again.

"I was so scared, Nana, I was the PP princess again," Roxy exclaimed. "The Pee Pee and Poo Poo Princess."

"All's well that ends well, Roxy. Thankfully, everyone is OK. Good thing Hunter was not with you, Eden's Uncle and Aunt would have skinned me alive if something happened to him!"

"Nana, you are the wind beneath my wings," Roxy answered. "Still, I need to walk around and calm down."

"OK, be careful," Nana said. "Hunter and I will stay here and take our naps. So Hunter, shall I put your jammies on and read you my lullaby?"

"Sleepy now, Nana," Hunter said.

"I love you so much, Hunter. You remind me of your Papa when he was your age. Sigh...time goes by so fast, I am a lucky Nana to spend time with my grand kiddos," Nana said with a tear in her eye.

"Lub you, Nana," Hunter mumbled.

"Good night my love good night..." Nana started the lullaby.

Chapter 4

Outside Roxy moved around the playground, noticing kids and dogs talking where flags were flying. Walking over, she stood quietly behind everyone. One of the young skiers noticed Roxy.

"Hey you, the one with the funny looking ear. I double dog dare you to put your tongue on that pole," he challenged Roxy. "Are you brave enough to do it?" he sneered to the group around the flagpole.

Roxy stood quietly shaking her head.

"I have an offer you can't refuse," he challenged. "See how long you can keep your tongue on the flagpole. It will impress all of us." Several kids snickered.

"Roxy, would you come here please," Nana called over the loudspeaker. "There is an emergency."

"Gotta go!" Roxy mumbled fleeing the crowd of kids.

"Are you chicken? Bawk Bawk!" someone yelled. "Can you hear out of that ear? It is so crooked, and looks funny. Come back here."

"No, I am choosing to leave now," Roxy answered.

"She is Cuckoo for Cocoa Puffs," another kid yelled.

"Is your Mommy calling you? What a big baby!"

Everyone was laughing as she ran away with her head hanging and her tail tucked between her legs.

"Bye Bye Chicken Little, Bye Bye Blackie. She is afraid and scared!" a third kid yelled from the crowd.

Roxy ran towards the lodge and the safety of Nana, with the cruel laughter ringing in her ears.

Chapter 5

Nana, Roxy and Hunter, sitting around the huge fireplace, were enjoying mugs of hot chocolate and marshmallows, while discussing what just happened to Roxy.

"Thank you, Nana, for helping me get out of that situation. Why don't some dogs and people like me? Because I have black fur? Because I look different?" Roxy puzzled Nana.

"I am so sorry to hear about this," Nana said. "I understand how you must feel. Humans have the same problems. I think people don't feel comfortable around someone different from them."

"Remember this," Nana declared, "You belong to an ancient blood line; you are an Affenpinscher. Feel the pride of your heritage!"

"Remember how you look on the OUTSIDE is not important. What defines a person is inside their heart, what is important is the person you are INSIDE," Nana continued. "Are you kind to others? Do you treat them with respect? Do you see the good in others? Do you help others? Don't you realize you are made for more?"

"Say what, Nana? Made for more? What does that mean?" Roxy asked.

"There is more to life than just me..." Nana said. "Another of my Life Lessons. We need to do more every day, beside thinking of just ourselves. The meaning of life is more than thinking of Me, Me, Me."

"But that is my favorite subject: Me," Roxy said. "Eden and Murphy feel the same way, maybe Toby and Coco too."

"I understand, but I am offering another way to think about the priorities in your life," Nana continued.

"But, I can't tell those big scary dogs who always smell my butt how to act," Roxy explained. "I'm too scared of them!"

"I know how you must feel, Roxy, it is a hard situation for sure. However, you can't tell others how to act or feel. All you can control is yourself."

"I'm in big trouble then. So, what is the answer, Nana?" Roxy inquired.

"It starts with a smile. It starts with your attitude, Roxy. You look those dogs in the eye. Tell them you are proud to be a black dog, an Affenpinscher. You love your crooked ear, it makes you special and unique. Then turn around and prance away with confidence. Like you did at the dog park in Sedona," Nana replied.

"Remember what Christopher Robin said," Nana told Roxy.

"You're braver than you believe. Stronger than you seem and smarter than you think."

"AS IF! Really?" Roxy questioned.

"Really," Nana said. "Treat others the way you want to be treated, another one of my Life Lessons. Maybe the next time they see you, they will treat you differently. You have all the answers to your questions and the solutions to your problems, inside your heart and mind. If it is to be, it is up to me, another of my Life Lessons."

"OOOkaaay, I will try it the next time," Roxy said.

"Good answer, great attitude," Nana replied.

"Remember when you were on the bow of the pirate ship? How you felt then? Bring that feeling back the next time you feel scared," Nana said.

"I am pup of the world." "I AM pup of the world."

"I AM PUP OF THE WORLD!" Roxy roared to the room.

"By jove, I think she's got it!" Nana said. "Let's stay nice and warm right in front of the fire until everyone gets back from skiing."

Chapter 6

Nana, in her bathrobe and curlers, Eden and Hunter in their pajamas, the dogs lying close to the fire, were discussing their day.

"Well, Hunter, did you enjoy being a part of the gang? Did you have fun? Do you want to join us again?" Nana asked as he sat on her lap.

"Nooooooo, Nana Nini," Hunter screamed. "Noooooooo. Want my Mama. Want my Papa. Want doggies."

"So glad to hear it," Nana swooned. "I love being surrounded by my family. Another almost perfect adventure and we had fun."

"Naannnaaa..."

"We nearly got buried alive in the snow, trying to help that bunny..."

"He called me a chicken, and it scared me.... They bullied me for--- "

"You got stuck in the gondola with your butt hanging out... You crashed and burned on the BUNNY slope..."

"I was so embarrassed. What if my friends saw me with you?"

"Hunter could barely move..."

"WE HAD FUN. Period. End of the story," Nana said.

"Yes, Nana, you're right Nana," Roxy said. "You're the Boss."

"I hear you cluckin' big Chicken," Nana beamed.

"Nana, never use that phrase around me," Roxy pleaded.

"Yes dear. Nana knows...you guys are AWESOME. I love you. Can't wait for our next perfect adventure."

Nana Knows You're... River-worthy

Chapter 1

"Who wants to go with me on a new adventure? See something special, for one of my kiddos?" Nana asked her grand kids. They were all sitting in Nana's great room in front of the large window, with the Superstition Mountains in view. Nana with her messy grey hair, was wearing her favorite outfit, her pleasantly plump figure, covered with dog hair. She filled the room with flea market finds contributing to a welcoming feeling.

"Ahhhh, I have too much homework, Nana. Can't do it today," Eden quickly replied. She was Nana's oldest grandchild. With medium length brown hair, blue-grey eyes and tons of freckles, she was wearing her favorite color, purple. Nana had a special love for her. She told Eden, "You're just too cute for words," many times. Eden was special because she was the only human girl in the bunch of kiddos.

"Oops, no can do," Murphy and Roxy said in unison. Nana's 'furry' grand kids, rescued from a shelter, were also adored by Nana. Murphy, a Dandie Dinmont mixed breed, always wagged his big bushy brown tail. Because he is super friendly, he has never met a stranger. Roxy, an Affenpinscher mixed breed, always has her black tail tucked between her legs as she is very shy and afraid of everything.

"Come on you guys, you know how much fun we have on our trips. Remember, I have a perfect record of no broken bones," Nana said.

"That may be true, but what about the time you---"

"You guys are so critical, you always focus on the negative, not the positive in a situation," Nana pouted.

"We love you, you're the best Nana ever! Especially when you buy us lots of presents," Eden explained.

"Yes, Nana we love all the walks you take us on, you're the bomb," Murphy said.

"Why do I feel like I have the Eddie Haskell trio in my living room?" Nana replied.

"Who? You always talk about these people we know nothing about," Murphy asked.

"Where do you want to go this time, Nana?" Eden asked.

"Did you ever hear of *Leave it to Beaver?* On TV? Whatever. This time we will do something just for Eden. Want to see wild horses?" Nana questioned.

"Awesome," Eden exclaimed.

"Not really, we get to ride your horses, Donny and Marie," Murphy declared.

"But these wild horses live by the lower Salt River on the Tonto National Forest just a few miles from where we are right now. After being there for centuries, people wanted to remove them and destroy them. But dedicated volunteers stopped that from happening, and now they belong to the state of Arizona. I like to go there and observe them and make sure they are safe and admire their beauty. Now they are protected by Arizona legislation," Nana explained to everyone.

"Big whoop."

"Eden, your great-great-grandparents may have seen them 100 years ago," Nana continued. "They used to go to the river to get away from the heat, with Great Grandpa when he was your age. I have loved tubing on the river for years. Your Papa and Uncle both loved to go here when they were young; so five generations of my family have enjoyed being by the river. The Tonto National Forest was built to form and protect the watersheds of the Salt and Verde rivers. Water is so important here in the desert. We all need to protect the quality of the water and the riparian area conditions. There are around 400 species of animals that live here."

"Double big whoop. So were you a toddler, like Hunter, 100 years ago?" Roxy asked.

"I have told you many times, I am not old, but 'seasoned,'" Nana pouted.

"Whoa, Nellie. Don't be so touchy," Murphy said.

"So are they like the horse, *Spirit*, on *Netflix*?" Eden questioned.

"Dude, it is totally awesome," Nana beamed to the kiddos.

"Count me in, Nana," Eden shouted. "I love horses!"

"Let's get ready for bed, so I can read you my lullaby," Nana suggested as they left the living room.

"I fear big animals, Nana, as you know," Roxy whispered.

Nana replied, "What happened to Roaring Roxy? Aren't you Pup of the World? Didn't you raise your paw to the sky and say you would never feel scared again?"

"Wellllll..., that was in the past," Roxy mumbled.

"You need to face your fears, Roxy. I know you can do this," Nana declared.

"All-righty then, we'll go tomorrow to enjoy a new adventure. I know this will be a perfect trip for us. Good night, I love you guys," Nana said as she tucked everyone into bed in Eden's room.

"Let me read to you.."

"Good night my love..."

After Nana read her lullaby to the gang and left the room, Murphy asked, "What are the chances we will have fun tomorrow with no problems?"

"Is there a number below zero?" Eden asked.

"Well, I will think of all the scary parts tomorrow. After all, tomorrow is another day...." Roxy sighed.

Chapter 2

The next morning everyone piled into the SUV and headed towards the lower Salt River. Eden named the vehicle the Moxymobile because it combined both of the names Murphy and Roxy. Loaded with Nana's 'must haves', including kayaks to float down the river, they also were pulling Nana's toy hauler with her ATV inside. This was a short wagon train compared to other trips the gang took with Nana. Still, the caravan careened down the road heading towards the river.

First, Nana and the kiddos stopped at Butcher Jones beach and rode the ATV on some trails. Nana was careful to stay on the designated trails, so they would not cause damage to the environment. Nana drove with Eden strapped in next to her. Murphy and Roxy were in the backseat. With the open sides of the ATV and the wind whipping at them, everyone held on for dear life. Nana zipped and zagged up and down the trails on the hills. In no time they were back to the start of the trail head.

"Eden, as your Papa once said, I had too much fun!" Nana yelled to the kiddos. "Want to go again?"

"Pass!" Everyone yelled in unison.

"As you wish, onward and upward then. Horses here we come." Nana exclaimed as the MM caravan zoomed out of the parking lot after reloading the ATV into the hauler.

When they got to the river everyone emptied items from the SUV on to the kayaks and entered the river with Nana on one kayak, her walker strapped to it. Murphy and Roxy were in another kayak and Eden had her own kayak. There was a fourth kayak filled with things needed for the trip down the river. There was a lot of drinking water for everyone, snacks, gloves, binoculars, cameras, a shovel, wire cutters, a first aid kit, food, whistles, maps, ropes and a pooper scooper. They looked like a floating wagon train slowly moving down the river. The female version of the Lewis and Clark expeditions, the *Sassy Salties*. Nana also thought of herself as Georgie White, riding the rapids on the Colorado river in the Grand Canyon.

The sky was a brilliant blue with large, puffy clouds. The Saguaros were marching up the bluffs with their arms reaching towards the sky. A band of horses were grazing near the bluff; eagles were flying in circles in the sky, sometimes diving into the water looking for fish. They could see egrets under the rushes. It was a lush garden, Arizona style, home to many species that shared their environment with humans.

"Ok, Nana, where are these wild horses?" Eden asked.

"Patience is a virtue," Nana replied, "Isn't this just heaven? So beautiful! See those cardinals? Doesn't this just put deposits in your emotional bank account? I love Arizona! We are so lucky to live here."

"What! Oh brother, I am bored already. This is just as boring as all the road trips we HAVE to go on with you," Eden pouted. "Where are these special horses?"

"Now, now. You know I want to be with you guys and have you all to myself, so I can teach you my Life Lessons," Nana beamed at her three amigos. "Nana Nini's my name, spoilin' kiddos my game."

"No, please no. NOT again. No more positive thoughts. Can I text on the river? Can I watch my videos?" Eden pouted even louder.

"Eden Lynne. Behave. This is all for you, because you love horses," Nana declared. "You will NOT be the first person to float down this river watching video games in a waterproof pouch! We are here to be in nature. To love the beauty all around us that God created. To have FUN and LOVE nature. NOW."

"Ok," Eden said with a big sigh. "However, I think I may throw up."

"See those cliffs, up ahead of us, Nana? I want to climb them and dive off." Murphy said. "That will add excitement to this trip."

"Locals call these bluffs the Bulldog cliffs. See how they kind of look like a bulldog laying down? Just like Snoopy in Sedona? Remember that trip? Don't climb too high," Nana advised.

"Well, just be careful and don't splash us," Eden advised. "You never know who might be around here. What if one of my friends saw me with you acting silly?"

"You are floating in water, you know. A little extra water should not hurt you," Murphy said feeling miffed.

"Saaalt Riiivver wider than a kayak... Nana sang at the top of her voice. "I'm crossing you in...style..."

"Nana, be quiet, you are scaring everyone and everything," Roxy said. "And it is BEYOND embarrassing."

"Okey Dokey, but they are used to the music. Mr. Mario sings opera while he works cleaning the grounds here on the river. Where else in the world can you get all this natural beauty while listening to Mozart?" Nana questioned. "All of this just feeds my soul. Cleaning toilets and singing with a beautiful voice like that? Magnifico!"

"Nana, Pleessseee.... that is beyond disgusting," Eden sniffed. "Does that make him the Pee and Poo Prince? Like Roxy is the Pee Pee and Poo Poo Princess?"

"Be nice," Nana replied.

"Can we catch these horses and ride them?" Eden asked.

"NO. The state protects them and the horses are not to be disturbed in any way."

"Still bored....." the gang said in unison.

"So we get to LOOK at them and nothing else?" Eden asked.

"I'm with Eden, bored, bored, bored," Roxy replied. "Nana, Eden's kayak just touched mine, on purpose!"

"Oh, eat SNAKE SNOT, Roxy," Eden snarled.

"There are snakes in this river? Nana, can I stop now and go back to the Moxymobile? Snakes may be smaller than me, but... they have fangs...and they are poisonous...and they rattle...and they have fangs!"

"Come on you guys, can't we all just get along? Where is your sense of adventure?" Nana asked.

"I think we have had enough 'adventure' with you, Nana. Remember the time---" Roxy replied.

"OK, OK. Watch out gang, here comes Murph."

Murphy dive-bombed right in front of Nana and caused her kayak to overturn and she kept coming up in her kayak repeatedly, making her feel very dizzy.

"Murphy, don't you look where you jump? Remember one of my Life Lessons is to follow the Golden Rule—treat others the way you would like to be treated?" Nana demanded. "You would not like it if someone did that to you."

"Sorry Nana, my bad," Murphy mumbled.

"Time to get out of this river and take a rest on the bank of the river," Nana said as the gang pulled their kayaks on the bank and hid them under the trees.

"Look, I see horses. Let's go," Eden yelled.

"Wait, be careful how you approach them," Nana said. "We need to stay 40 to 50 feet away from them. That is about the length of a school bus." "Can't we go up to them and pet them? Can't we lasso them like we did the coyote pup?" Murphy asked as he shook all the water off his furry coat.

"I want to ride one, they are so beautiful," Eden whispered. "Amy Fleming could ride them."

"I told you they are protected and must be treated with respect. They are wild and free. Don't look them in the eye and don't walk towards them," Nana said. "We need to walk at an angle and make no loud noises or movements."

"Look at that one, she has a necklace on! Why would a wild horse have on a necklace?" Eden questioned. "I wish I could take tons of pictures."

"That is a mystery for sure," Nana said. "It looks like it might be an amethyst stone. Maybe it is from the amethyst mine in the Four Peaks region.

"Is there a mine here like the Lost Dutchman mine?" Murphy questioned.

"It is a working mine where people can remove amethyst stones. The only way to get there is via helicopter," Nana explained. "See that mountain range with the four peaks?" Nana pointed to a mountain range not too far from the river. On a clear day the range was visible like a mirror on the Salt river.

"Totally awesome," Murphy said.

Eden was looking at the horses with the binoculars still strapped around Nana's neck.

"Why don't we go up to her quietly, and ask her how she got the necklace around her neck?"

"These horses don't talk like you guys," Nana said. "These animals have always been here. It is so wonderful they can stay here in their habitat and be safe. They are wild animals and this is their home. It is like being right in the middle of the Salt River Wild Animal Zoo! We are so lucky to come here any time we want."

"Can't you feed them the magic flowers we ate from Costa Rica?"

Murphy asked. "Remember Eden's Uncle brought them to us and now we can talk."

"No, that is not an option," Nana explained. "Not all animals can talk like you guys."

"But, I want to know how that horse could get a purple necklace out here in the boonies," Eden explained. "How can we solve this mystery?"

"The old-fashioned way. We will follow them and look for clues and use our minds to figure this mystery out," Nana explained. "We need to look at all the pieces of the puzzle and fit them together to get the big picture."

"So, with all the stuff you brought, did you bring a CSI kit like on TV?" Roxy asked. "Isn't one of your Life Lessons: prior planning prevents poor performance?"

"True," Nana explained. "But, I somehow did not bring the kit."

"Nana Nini! Now, what do we do?" Eden replied.

"Remember, another of my Life Lessons: if it is to be, it is up to me," Nana said. "So we'll just have to figure out this mystery, using our hands, eyes and our mind. We will look for clues and use them to see if they can explain this puzzle. Why does a wild horse in the middle of nowhere have a beautiful purple necklace around her neck?"

"We are doomed.....Remember how we 'solved' the mystery of the gold in the Superstitions?" Roxy questioned.

"I think you mean didn't solve the mystery?" Eden questioned. "Maybe this time will be different."

Chapter 3

Nana and the gang followed the horses by the hoofprints in the sand and the broken branches of the trees. When the horses stopped and rested by the river, Nana and the kiddos watched them hidden in the brush.

"How could anyone kill these beautiful animals? They are not hurting anyone," Nana asked the kiddos. "They are an icon of the wild, free spirits of the American West," Nana explained.

"What is an i-i-i cone?" Roxy asked. "Do you mean they eat ice cream?"

"Not ice cream! And that is i-c-o-n and means someone or something has a special meaning for a person or place," Nana explained.

"Look over there, everyone. And you call me the Pee Pee and Poo Poo Princess!" Roxy said. "I have never seen so much poop in my life."

"Here a poop, there a poop, everywhere a poop, poop! Old Nana Nini has a scooper, ei ei oh..." Nana sang.

"Again, totally embarrassing, Nana," Eden said. "And gross. Please don't sing."

"Tisk, Tisk, Tisk. It is good for their habitat. The horses eat the grass and then pass it back to the earth through their poop," Nana replied. "They call that large pile a Stud Pile. This is another clue to track the horses. Follow their poop," Nana declared.

"Yuck. Is that an icon??" Eden laughed. "Mountains of poop everywhere along the river?"

"Ha, Ha, hilarious," Nana laughed too.

"At least I have my cameras," Nana said. "Finally, bringing all my stuff has been beneficial. Look over there, do you guys see...? Oh my goodness, those are so adorable. Look, do you see them?"

Chapter 4

"Nana. What are they?" The gang asked.

"Those are river otters and differ from sea otters like the ones where you live in California, Eden," Nana explained.

"They are just as adorable and they are holding hands," Eden observed.

"A mother and her pup hold hands so they don't float away from each other," Nana further explained.

"Anyway, Nana, you have too much stuff," Roxy said. "We do not use it on our adventures."

"Hey now, remember when Eden had her whistle and saved you and helped you guys with rescuing the rabbit in the cave after the avalanche in Colorado?" Nana asked. "My stuff came in handy then."

"Whateverrrr."

"Wait, I see a big box high in a tree over there," Nana yelled.

"Shuushh! Be quiet, don't startle the horses," Eden cautioned.

"Sorry, I got excited," Nana replied. "How did that box get up there? What is in it? How do we find out what is in there without scaring the horses? Is it important to our mystery? Oh, I feel like Nan Bobbsey!"

"Who?"

"You know from the books, The *Bobbsey Twins*? Or *Nancy Drew*?" Nana said.

"Again, who?" Murphy asked.

"It makes me feel more like Indiana Jones," Murphy said.

"I am Eden the Explorer, just like Dora," Eden said.

"How about we are like Clifford the Big Red Dog?" Roxy said. "This could be fun! Or Blue from Blue's Clues."

"Anyway," Nana said. "I think the box is an important clue. How did it get up there? We need to see what is inside it. Roxy, you are the smallest, go quietly climb that tree and see what is inside it, please. And watch out for snakes and bees and red ants and tarantula hawks and bobcats and javelinas and coyotes."

"NANA, you know I don't like heights and being brave and especially anything that crawls," Roxy pouted.

"Put on your Big Girl Panties and do it," Nana demanded.

"I would need your HUGE Granny panties to make me brave enough to do that," Roxy mumbled.

"Whatever floats your kayak," Nana said.

"How will I get down? What if I scare the horses and they stampede?"

"Roxy, remember you are the solutions to your problems and the answers to your questions," Nana explained. "If it is to be, it is up to me."

"How would any of these other heroes solve this?" Nana questioned. "Put on your thinking caps and give me a solution to Roxy's problem."

"Jump until you reach a branch and shake it, or saw down the branch holding it?" Murphy offered. "I know, Roxy, why don't you tie the rope to the box and sit on it and gravity will slowly bring you down?"

"Good answer," Eden said.

"Wish me luck, here I go," Roxy quietly mumbled.

Roxy took the rope Nana handed her, and put it around her neck. She climbed up the tree. She then tied the rope around the box, wrapping it around the branch of the tree. Roxy carefully sat on the top of the box and slowly lowered everything down to the sand.

"What is inside this box? Is it treasure similar to the gold in the Superstitions? Maybe it came off of Cap'n Jack Sparrow's pirate ship?" Murphy asked.

"I did it!! I kept saying to myself, I was PUP of the World like before and I was not scared," Roxy beamed.

"See, I knew you could do it, Roaring Roxy. This time you were a Sassy Saltie," Eden replied. "So how did it get on Plum's neck? I named her that because of the purple necklace."

The gang stood looking at the open box, containing some rusty and dirty jewelry, among some rocks and dirt, with a large hole in the bottom.

"Maybe there was a flood a long time ago. The water from it settled in the tree and the chest landed up there? The necklace fell out of the hole and just landed on her neck? Possibly from the amethyst mine, you told us about?" Eden questioned Nana and the two dogs.

"I think you found a good solution for how it happened. We will never know for sure. Good job everyone," Nana said. "My smart babies. I love you guys. We figured out the mystery by using our minds and following the signs and clues. Old-fashioned reasoning wins the day. Just like on **Dateline** or **48 Hours**."

"As if, Nana," Eden said. "And I was just guessing too, Nana."

"That is OK, Eden. Sometimes guessing has a lot to do with solving mysteries," Nana explained. "Some people call that brainstorming; thinking of options of how something may have happened."

"So can we take this stuff and sell it and make a lot of money and buy lots of toys? FINALLY, we will be rich and famous," Murphy yelled. "Sorry no fool's gold this time, money, money, money!"

"No, this booty belongs to the horses. We will take it and donate it to the volunteers, who support these animals," Nana said. "These volunteers are amazing. They do whatever is necessary to protect these horses. A big problem is the horses getting hit by cars on the road. The money from this treasure can be the start to solving this problem; building under or overpasses to keep the horses away from the road. Remember, one of my Life Lessons is we are made for more. There is more to life than just me."

"But Nana!! Really? We solved the mystery! That's not fair," Murphy pouted.

"EXCUSE me, I rescued the chest," Roxy said. "I deserve ALL the money."

"Murphy, Roxy, we want to do the right thing," Nana explained. "This does not belong to us. Remember, we want to treat others the way we would want to be treated."

Eden said, "I was the one who solved the mystery of the box. I should get all the money with pictures of me everywhere."

"Eden..."

"We can tell them how brave Roxy was to get the box down from the tree," Nana said.

"I was Roaring Roxy again."

"I was Excellent Eden again."

"I was Mighty Murph again."

"I was Nifty Nana. We can post it all on *Facebook* and tell them about the time---"

"Nana, can we post pictures for my friends to see, and make a *You Tube* video starring ME?"

"EeeeDDDDeenn!!"

Nana Knows You're... Sleep-worthy

Good night my love, good night.
Sweet dreams my love,
Showered in the moonlight.
Time for sleep tonight.
Mr. Sandman, do not fight.
You've had a busy day, now is the time to rest.
Tomorrow you want to be your best.

So, take a deep breath...
Let it go as you think...
I am thankful.
With the love that surrounds me.
I am content.
With the love that surrounds me.

Take another deep breath...
Let it go as you think...
I am thankful.
For the adults in my life who support me.
I am grateful.
For the adults in my life who support me.

Take another deep breath...
Let it go as you think...
I am thankful.
For my strong and healthy body.
I am grateful.
For my strong and healthy body.

Take another deep breath...
Let it go as you think...
I am thankful.
For my family.
I am appreciative.
Of my family.

Take another deep breath...
Let it go as you think...
I am grateful.
For my friends.
I am blessed.
With my friends.

Now take another deep breath...
Let it go as you think...
I am thankful.
With the beauty all around me.
I am present.
With the beauty all around me.

Take a very deep breath...
And let it go as you think...
I am thankful.

With the feeling of peace.
I am blessed.
With the feeling of peace.

Take another deep breath...
Let it go as you think...
I am thankful.
With my Heavenly Father who loves me.
I am at peace.
With He who loves me.

Take a deep breath...
Let it go as you think...
Tonight I am blessed.
Tonight I am thankful.
Tonight I am grateful.
Tonight I am at peace.
Tonight I am safe and content.

For everything in my life.
And I ask for these gifts to fill my tomorrows.

Good night my love, good night.
Sweet dreams my love, tonight.
You're adored, loved and cherished.
Good night my love, good night.
I Love You.
Forever and Always, Nana

About the Author:

Susan Edie, a second generation Arizona native, graduated from Arizona State University. She has had an eclectic career, including as a substitute teacher. She loved reading stories to students and a book idea about Nana Nini grew from their enthusiasm. Her granddaughter loves her dogs, Murphy and Roxy, they are central to the stories. This is Susan's first attempt at creative writing, taking on-line courses, seminars and workshops; including as a member of the Society of Children Book Writer's and Illustrators.

Ms. Ashe spends time outdoors, enjoying Arizona's adventures. With her interior design background, she finds treasures for her home rewarding. She also enjoys helping others, having volunteered at various charities.

She lives in Mesa, Arizona with Roxy, the PP Princess. She practices her life lessons on her two sons and three grandchildren.

She can be reached on her website: susanedieashe.com

DON'T ever let ANYONE DULL your Sparkle

Printed in the United States
By Bookmasters